A Night in the
Dinosaur Graveyard

WRITTEN BY A. J. WOOD
ILLUSTRATED BY WAYNE ANDERSON

TEMPLAR

On Max and Lucy's first fossil hunt, their grandfather,
Professor Sponge, led them to an old gravestone by a stream.

"Children," he said solemnly, "this is the grave of a famous
fossil hunter who died here mysteriously many years ago.
No one knows exactly what happened to him."

Suddenly, Soap started barking furiously. He had found
a bone—the biggest bone the professor had ever seen.
It gave off a strange light.

R.I.P.
Dr DIGGER
JUNE 3ʳᵈ 1885

"It's getting late," said the professor.
"Let's get a good night's rest and in
the morning we'll see what else we
can find."

They camped for the night in a cave in the
mountainside. It was dark and cold.

All of a sudden, a ghostly silver shape
appeared on the other side of the cave.
Soap barked loudly, waking the professor.

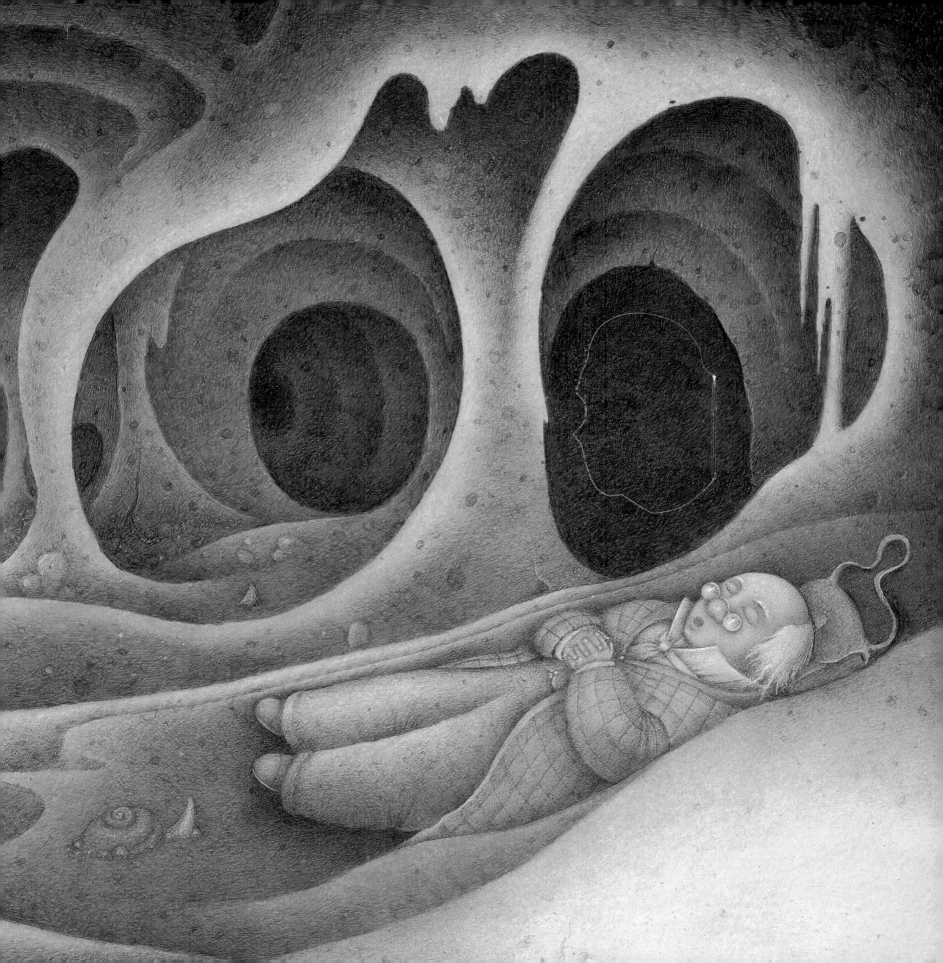

"They're monsters!" yelled Max.
"They're gh-gh-ghosts!" chattered Lucy.
"They're dinosaurs!" exclaimed the professor.
The dinosaur ghosts floated above and behind
them, glowing and groaning horribly.

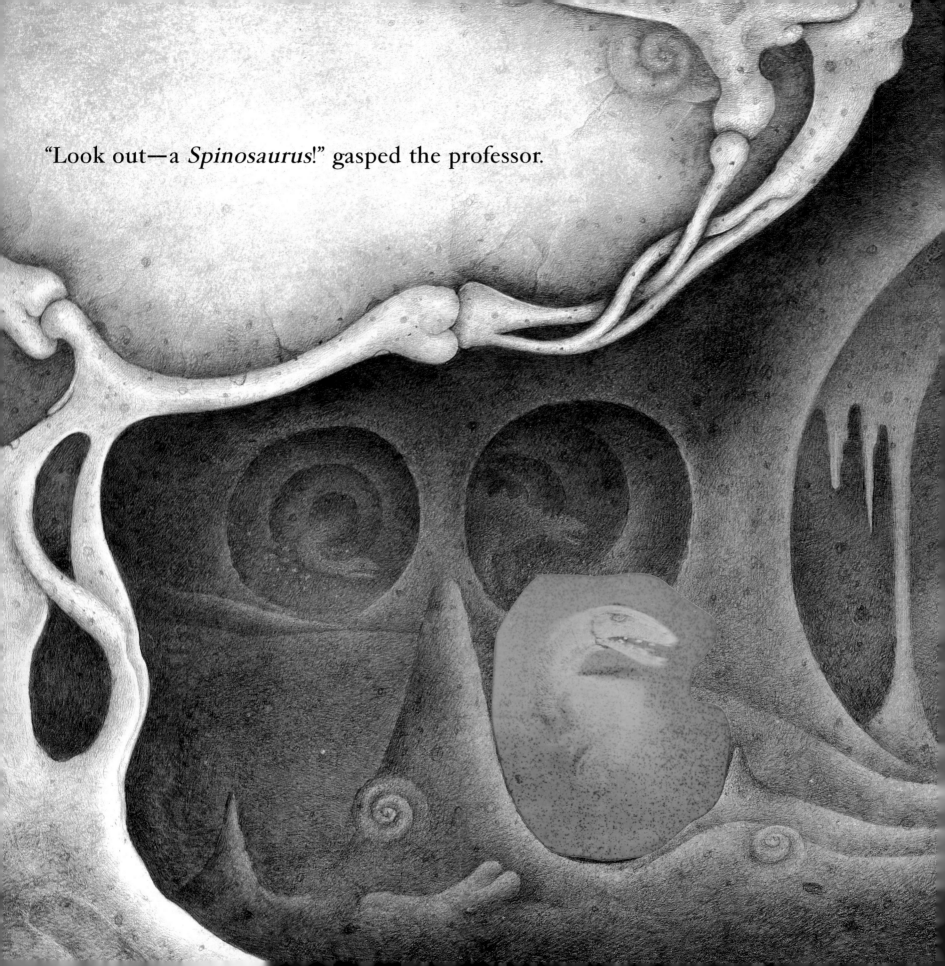

"Look out—a *Spinosaurus*!" gasped the professor.

On and on they ran, until . . .
"Oh, no—a dead end!" cried Lucy.

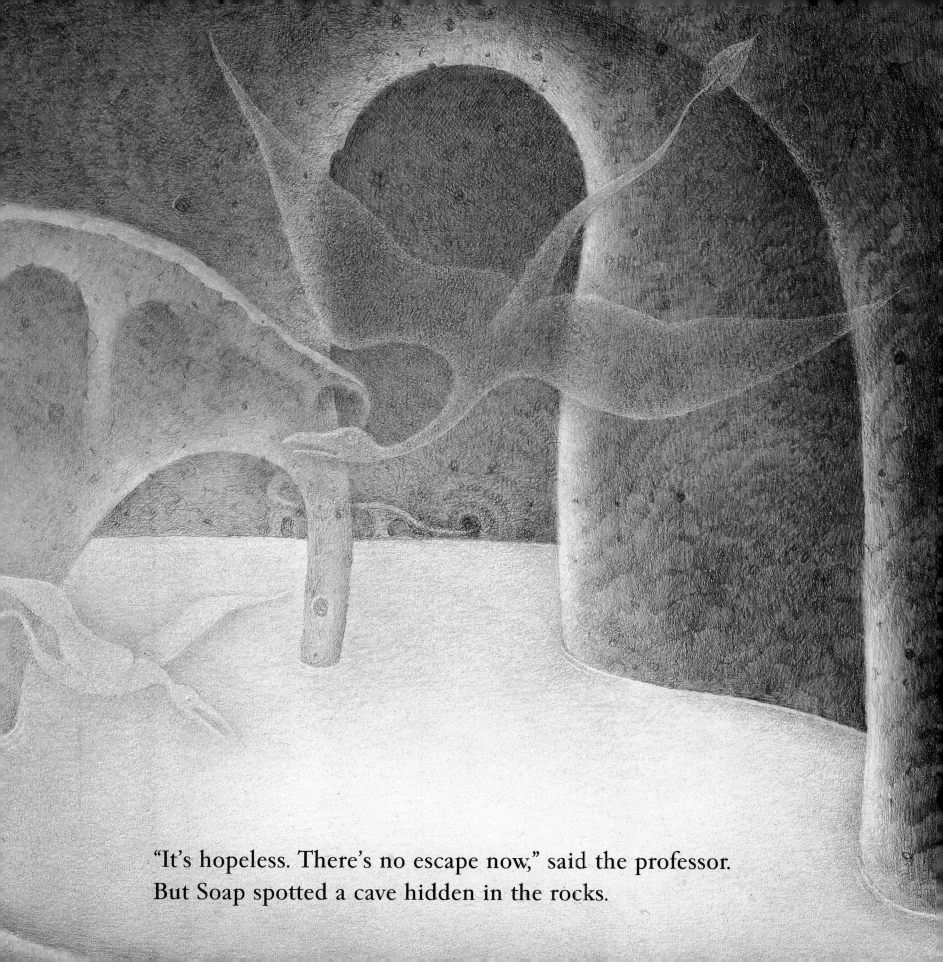

"It's hopeless. There's no escape now," said the professor.
But Soap spotted a cave hidden in the rocks.

"It looks like we've lost them.
Let's rest while we can," panted
the professor, as he leaned
against a boulder.

With a loud rumble, the boulder shifted, revealing a huge cavern full of skeletons and bones, lit by an eerie light. All of the dinosaur ghosts suddenly appeared before them.

They were trapped!

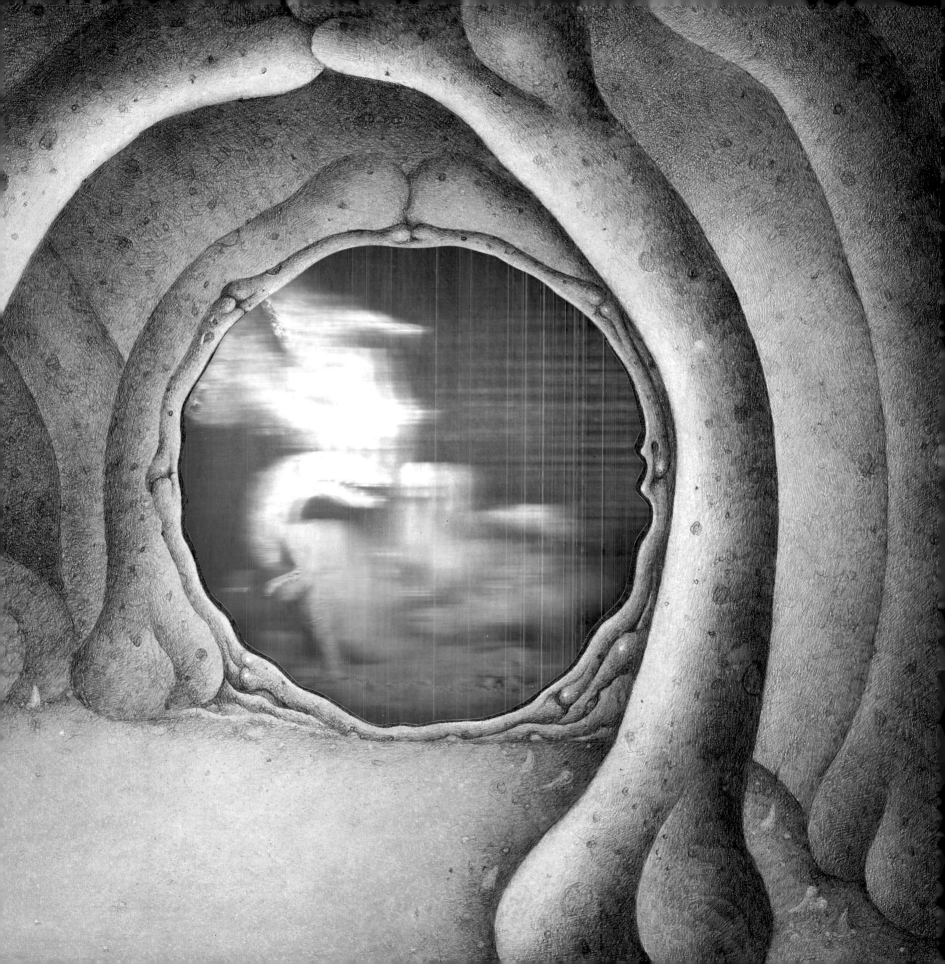

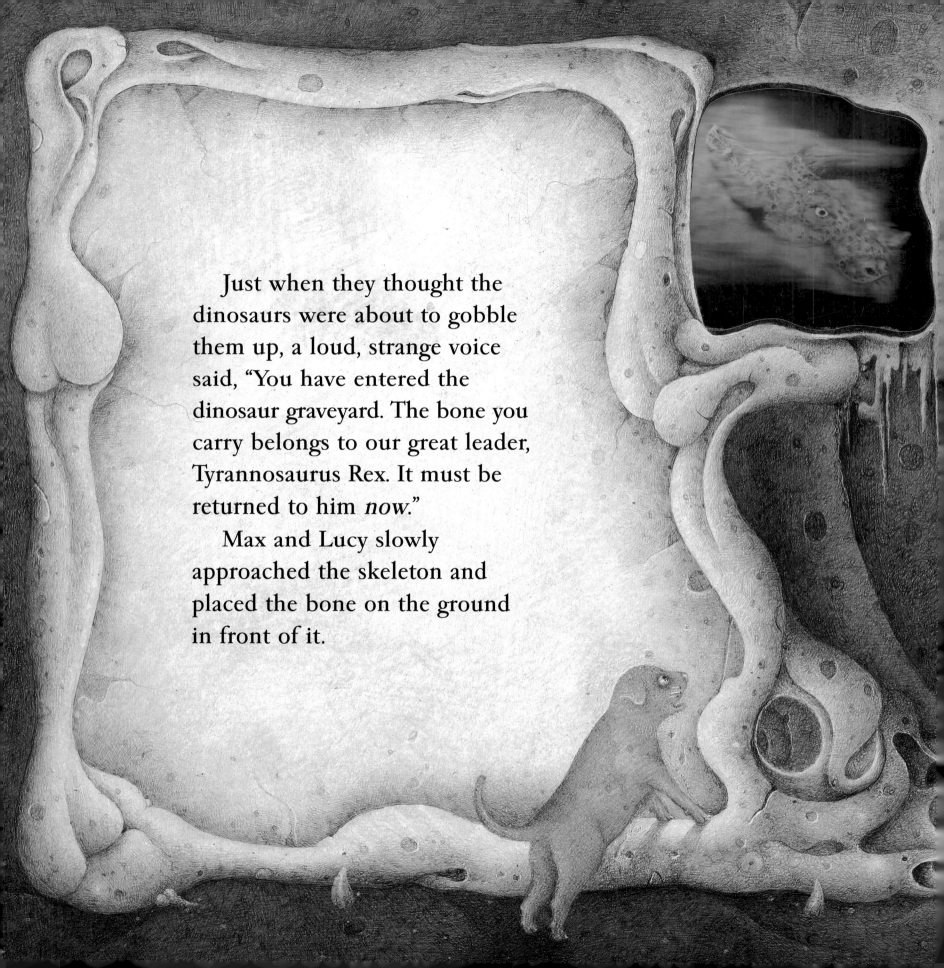

Just when they thought the dinosaurs were about to gobble them up, a loud, strange voice said, "You have entered the dinosaur graveyard. The bone you carry belongs to our great leader, Tyrannosaurus Rex. It must be returned to him *now*."

Max and Lucy slowly approached the skeleton and placed the bone on the ground in front of it.

As soon as they did, the skeleton
came to life.

"I am Tyrannosaurus Rex," it said.
"Ever since a wretched fossil
thief stole that bone from me,
I have been trapped here.
You have freed me at last.
I am forever grateful."

And with that, the
dinosaur ghosts
disappeared.